SAM'S SUPER SEATS

To my niece, Eveyah, may your love for reading last a lifetime.
—K.B.

To my son, Grey, who reminds me how important rest is.
—S.M.

KOKILA
An imprint of Penguin Random House LLC, New York

First published in the United States of America by Kokila, an imprint of Penguin Random House LLC, 2022

Text copyright © 2022 by Keah Brown
Illustrations copyright © 2022 by Sharee Miller

Kokila & colophon are registered trademarks of Penguin Random House LLC.
Visit us online at penguinrandomhouse.com.

Library of Congress Cataloging-in-Publication Data is available.

Manufactured in China

ISBN 9780593323892

1 3 5 7 9 10 8 6 4 2
TOPL

Design by Jasmin Rubero
Text set in Kievit Serif

The art for this book was created with pencil and watercolor on watercolor paper, and polished in Photoshop.

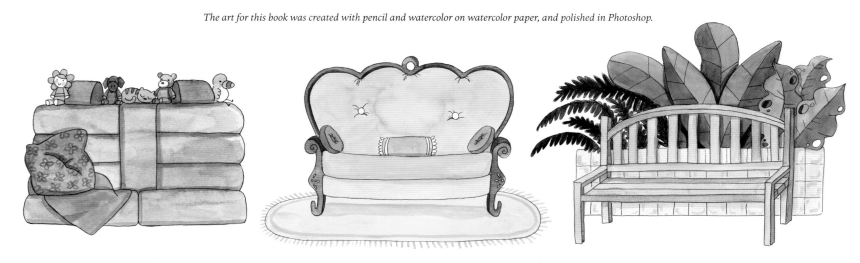

SAM'S SUPER SEATS

by **Keah Brown** 🖤 *illustrated by* **Sharee Miller**

Kokila

Hi! My name is Sam, and I love to make people laugh.

I love myself.

And I love to learn.

Today, I'm going to my favorite place for back-to-school shopping with my best friends, Sydney and Sarah.

Daddy helps me get ready so Mommy can sleep in before he heads to work.

We brush our teeth, sing songs into our hairbrushes, and after Daddy combs my hair, we do something super fun. Every morning, we say four things we like about me into the mirror.

Today, I like my dance skills, my eyes, and my fingers too.

"And, today, your smile is my favorite thing about you," Daddy says.

He's right.
It is pretty great.

Mommy is up now, getting dressed.
I can hear her singing.

"What does a ghost say when he is upset?"
I ask as Daddy gives me a piggyback ride
downstairs to the living room.
"I don't know. What?"
"This is unboolieveable!"
Daddy laughs and says goodbye with a
forehead kiss.

Before Mommy and I leave, I'm busy resting with my favorite super seat: Misty!

I have cerebral palsy, so I know that when my legs get tired I have to stop and sit.

Yesterday at the park, I overdid it on the swings, and my right leg still hurts a little.

Misty is the living room couch named after my favorite dancer, Misty Copeland. When we aren't doing pirouettes before dance class, we play "I spy" and laugh at our silly answers. Misty loves to dance, and I know she loves me. She's comfortable and graceful. That's what makes her a super seat.

"Ready to go?" Mommy asks. Misty wishes me well with a wink and a smile, and I promise her a rematch with a wave and a smile of my own.

My second favorite super seat is in the back of Mommy's car.
Whenever we go anywhere, I get to hang out with Laney. We
share secrets, and she always has a joke ready to make me laugh.

Laney makes me feel important and safe. She is funny, cool, and kind.

That's why she is a super seat of mine.

Laney cracks another joke when Sarah and Sydney crawl into the car. We laugh and laugh, and Mommy asks us, "What's so funny?"

"Nothing!" we say before laughing again.

At the mall, we see cute shirts, cute pants and skirts, and cute shoes.

My favorite colors are pink and blue, Sydney's are green and purple, and Sarah really likes orange and brown.

We are going to look so cute when we go back to school, because we've got brains *and* beauty.

Cuteness isn't just about clothes. It's about feeling good on the inside and outside, feeling strong, and feeling ready to learn.

Sarah, Sydney, and I walk around the mall with Mommy,

and she helps us put together two outfits each.

Sarah poses in front of the mirror, her orange shirt and sunflower-covered overalls shining under the light, like the models in magazines she wants to be. She is quiet but confident and loves clothes as much as me.

"I feel strong," she says.

"You look strong," I reply.

"I feel good," Sydney says.

"You look so cute," I reply.

I walk the runway, limping with pride with my left hand on my hip. I love the way I feel, like I could fly. I show off my jean skirt with pink hearts by the pockets and matching pink jacket while Sydney stands next to Mommy, pretending to take pictures with her hands. Her blue jeans and green sweater with stars on the sleeves remind me of all the stylish photographers she looks up to.

Sarah, Sydney, Mommy, and me pose and play pretend
before we are all in a pile on the floor, giggling.

We buy friendship bracelets, and Sydney helps me tie mine
around my wrist.

"Thank you," I say before we group hug.

"Let's wear these on the first day back to school," Sarah says.

We all high-five.

I love my friends. They help me when it's hard to do things and cheer me up with hugs when I am sad about it being hard. When they're sad, I like to make them laugh.

Going back to school is going to be so much fun.

After walking so much, my legs start to ache and tingle, like they fell asleep. That's how I know that I'm tired. I want to walk and run and play all day, but sometimes a little rest goes a long way.

"I am tired. I need to stop," I say.

Mommy smiles and says, "Me too. It's been a long day."

We stand still, holding hands while we look for a place to sit.

Mommy spots a place before the rest of us.

"Girls, let's go sit on that bench over there," she says.

And so we do.
We sit down and take some pictures with silly faces
and some with big smiles.

The bench is not a super seat yet because we are still strangers and its hard wood pokes my legs.

"Hi, I'm Maya," the bench says. "I know I'm not that comfy, but I can help you rest when you're tired."

"Thank you," I tell Maya. "But maybe next time you could ask to get pillows?"

I am still tired, but I won't be forever. "I will only be a few more minutes," I say.

"Take your time. People watching is fun!" Sydney says. Mommy squeezes my hand like she does when she wants me to remember that she loves me. I remember. I love her too.

We watch lots of people, and we see other kids with their families back-to-school shopping like us.

I can't wait to sit at a new desk and rest while we learn about places, people, and things. I can't wait to meet a new super seat.

To keep shopping, I'll need to rest here for a while, with my friends, Mommy, new clothes, and a super seat in training.

But then, I have one of the best ideas I've had all day.

When we get home, we sit on Misty
while Mommy grabs jewelry for us to try on from her room.

She comes back with rings, necklaces,
and barrettes for our hair. My space buns are
perfect, so I grab a ring. Sarah and Sydney
take some time to decide.

I look at myself in the mirror Mommy brought downstairs.

When I'm done, I see Sarah with two necklaces
and Sydney with barrettes on either side of her curly brown hair.

We all take turns looking in the mirror again. Today, I like my dance skills, my eyes, and my fingers too. What I like most about myself every day, though, is that I'm me. It isn't always easy, but being me is the best, and sometimes I need a little rest.